Oréan Collier was born in Frankfurt, Germany. She is an artist creating works using mixed media acrylic and watercolor. Her love for painting began while living in Hawaii for three years where she graduated high school. She always had a love for creating things, such as designing handbags, fabric design, sewing, and knitting. Oréan was chosen as the "Be Discovered" designer handbag contest winner with Marie Claire magazine with her winning design that was named after her late grandmother "Lillian." Oréan now resides in Chattanooga, Tennessee.

Ordering Information
Quantity sales: Special discounts are available on quantity purchases by corporations, associations, and others. For details, contact the publisher at the address below.

Publisher's Cataloging-in-Publication data
Collier,Oréan
Lasko The Artist

ISBN 9781647501952 (Paperback)
ISBN 9781647509118 (Hardback)
ISBN 9781647509125 (ePub e-book)

Library of Congress Control Number: 2021905676

www.austinmacauley.com/us

First Published (2021)
Austin Macauley Publishers LLC
40 Wall Street, 33rd Floor, Suite 3302
New York, NY 10005
USA

mail-usa@austinmacauley.com
+1 (646) 5125767

This book is lovingly dedicated to my beautiful one and only daughter, London D'Shai Collier, whose smile would light up any room, and to my two beautiful granddaughters, Lennox and Zari.

Thank you to my parents for always being there for me, never letting me forget to keep believing in myself and in my dreams. I would like to thank my beautiful daughter, London, who inspired me every day. You are always on my mind and forever in my heart.

v

Lasko the squirrel is a bit of a practical joker, who loves to play pranks but he also loves to paint. However, on this day he is all out of ideas on what to paint. So he goes to his mom to see if she has any ideas.

"I know," she says. "What about painting your friends?"
"Thanks, Mom, that's a great idea. I'm going outside, I'll see you later."
"Have fun!" says Mom.

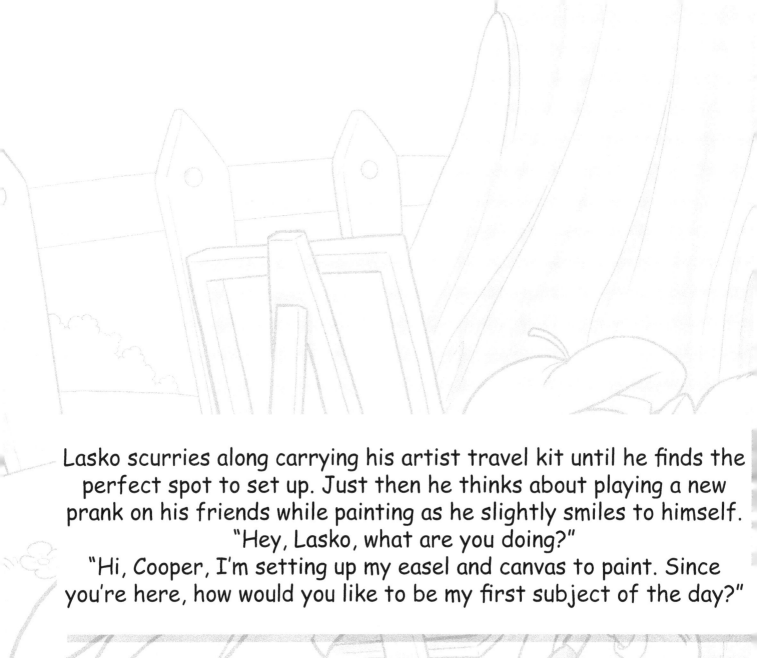

Lasko scurries along carrying his artist travel kit until he finds the
perfect spot to set up. Just then he thinks about playing a new
prank on his friends while painting as he slightly smiles to himself.
"Hey, Lasko, what are you doing?"
"Hi, Cooper, I'm setting up my easel and canvas to paint. Since
you're here, how would you like to be my first subject of the day?"

"Oh, OK sure, but what do I do?" asks Cooper.
"Go home and put your best outfit on and come back here so I can paint a picture of you."
"Sounds like fun, I'll see you in a few minutes," says Cooper.
Off goes Cooper to change into his fancy clothes.

"Lasko! I'm back!" shouts Cooper.
"Awesome, stand right over there by that old fence and don't move," instructs Lasko.

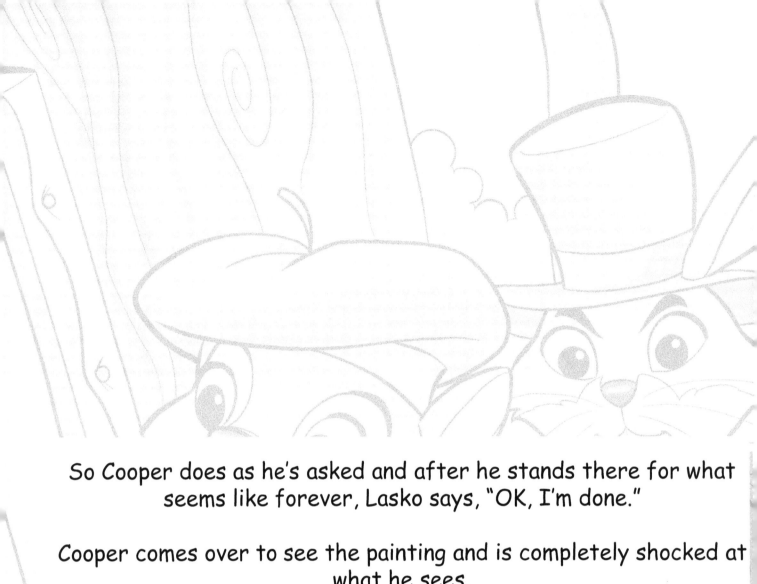

So Cooper does as he's asked and after he stands there for what seems like forever, Lasko says, "OK, I'm done."

Cooper comes over to see the painting and is completely shocked at what he sees.

"Lasko," says Cooper. "That's not a painting of me, that's you!"

"I know but isn't it good?" asks Lasko.
Cooper is so mad, he turns around in a huff and goes home.

Lasko stays there just admiring his work, when he looks up and sees his friend Izzy.

"Hey, Izzy!"
"Hi, Lasko, what are you doing?" asks Izzy.
"Well, I'm painting today," replies Lasko.
"What are you painting?" asks Izzy.
"I was thinking I could paint a picture of you."
"Me? Really, Lasko?" asks Izzy.
"Sure, why not," replies Lasko.

"Just go home and put your best outfit on and come ba..."
Before he can finish, Izzy is already running home to change into her favorite outfit.

Izzy returns to where Lasko is set up and says,
"I'm ready!"

"Great!" says Lasko. "Stand right over there,"
pointing to the old fence.

Izzy goes to pose for Lasko, showing how excited she is, and she can't wait to see the end result.

Before you know it, Lasko says, "I'm finished."
Izzy comes right over to see the painting and when she does, she
cannot believe it.

"Lasko, that's not me, that's you!" says Izzy.
"I know but isn't it good!" replies Lasko.

The smile is nowhere on Izzy's face, she quickly turns in a
huff and leaves.

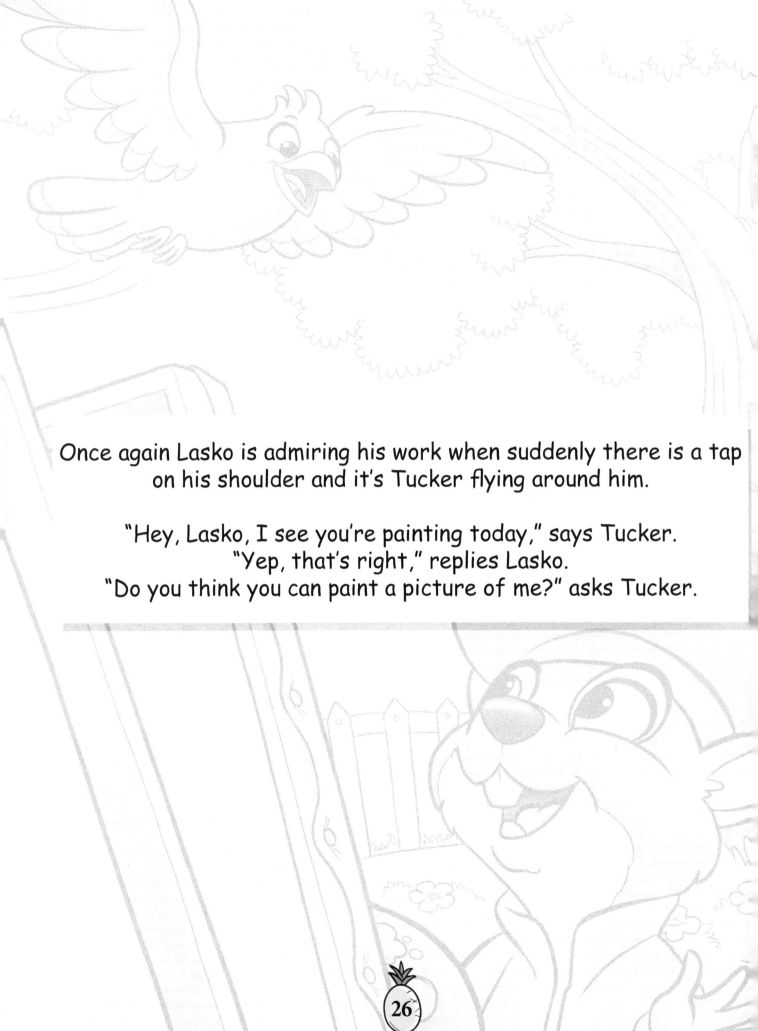

Once again Lasko is admiring his work when suddenly there is a tap on his shoulder and it's Tucker flying around him.

"Hey, Lasko, I see you're painting today," says Tucker.
"Yep, that's right," replies Lasko.
"Do you think you can paint a picture of me?" asks Tucker.

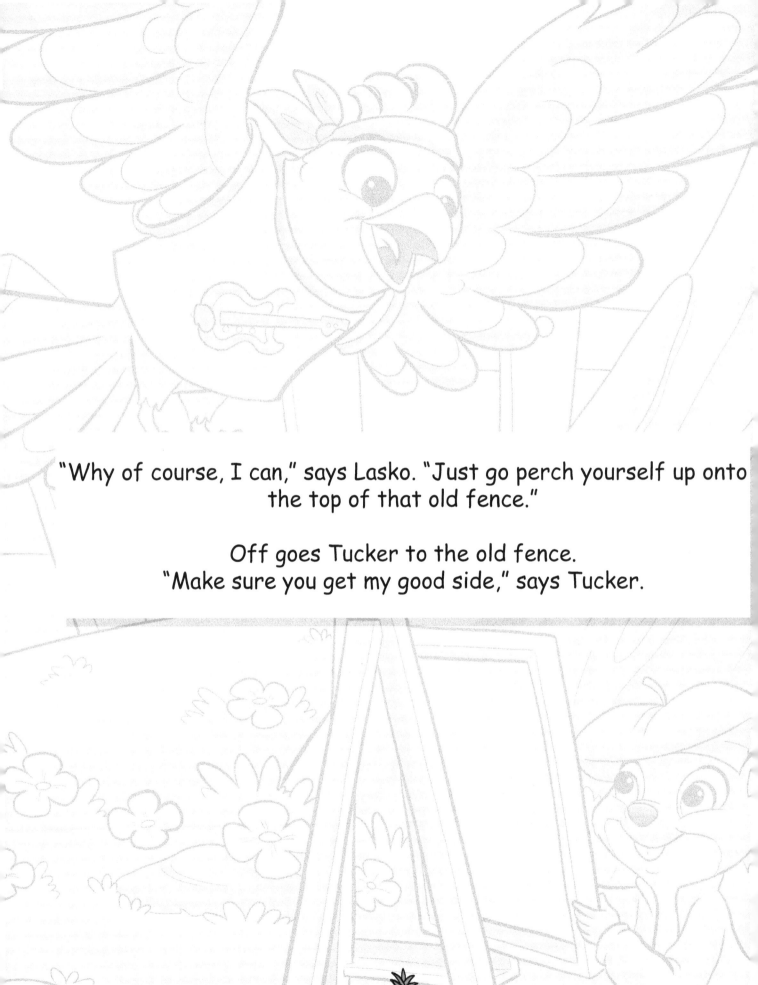

"Why of course, I can," says Lasko. "Just go perch yourself up onto the top of that old fence."

Off goes Tucker to the old fence.
"Make sure you get my good side," says Tucker.

As some time passes by, Lasko finally puts down his paint brush. Tucker flies over to see the painting.

Lasko says, "Ta-da!"
Tucker looks at the painting, then looks back at Lasko, then back at the painting.

"Well, clearly that's not me, that's you, Lasko!" sighs Tucker.

Lasko replies, "I know but isn't it good?"
Tucker flies away in a huff.

Lasko then begins to pick up all his art and art supplies
and heads home.

On the way he sees Cooper, Izzy, and Tucker all playing together.
So he stops to ask if he can play too.
They all shout in a loud voice at the same time,
"NO!"
They run and fly away from Lasko, leaving him all alone.
Lasko becomes really sad and when he gets home, he tells his
mommy what happened. To which she replies, "Lasko, you're telling
me that you invited all your friends to put on their best outfits and
pose for pictures and you didn't paint them,
you painted yourself instead?"

"Yes, Mommy," says Lasko with a faint voice.
"Oh my, Lasko, that simply was not very nice at all. No wonder they
are upset with you," sighs Mommy.

"What should I do, Mommy?" asks Lasko.
"Well, you should think about your actions and come up with a
solution of how you can make things right again with your friends.
I'll leave you to it."
"Yes, Mommy, I will," says Lasko.

Lasko really does feel bad about how he handled things. He decides
to go outside and walk around for a minute to think.

Once outside he sees up the road a bit, how much fun Cooper, Izzy, and Tucker are having. So he thinks what about if he paints one big painting of all of them together, just playing and enjoying themselves.

So off goes Lasko to get his art supplies and quickly sets up a spot away from where they might notice him.

Lasko begins to paint Cooper and Izzy playing catch while Tucker is flying and darting in and out all around them.

Right when he finishes the painting, Tucker notices him and says, "Hey, there's Lasko."
Just then they all begin to leave when Lasko notices and shouts, "WAIT!"

He quickly runs toward them holding his finished piece, when Cooper replies, "Sorry, Lasko, we don't have time for any more pranks."
"No, no, Cooper," replies Lasko. "This is not a prank, I was wrong earlier and I wanted to say sorry and make it up to you guys."
"So what is it?" asks Tucker.
"Voi-la!" exclaims Lasko.

He turns the painting around so everybody can see it.
They all look at the painting and begin to smile with joy.
They love it.

"Wow! It's beautiful, Lasko," says Izzy.
"Thanks, guys, I hope you can forgive me."
They all reply, "Of course, we can."
"Now let's ALL go play," and off they go.

CPSIA information can be obtained
at www.ICGtesting.com
Printed in the USA
LVHW071427060521
686679LV00016B/462